BOI

For Mum, who has taught us all
a thing or two about bouncing back — Sean T

For Bumpy

A big thanks to Daniel! — Bruce

Text copyright © 2004 by Sean Taylor
Illustrations copyright © 2004 by Bruce Ingman

First U.S. edition 2004

Library of Congress Cataloging-in-
Publication Data is available.

Library of Congress Catalog Card
Number 2003065222

ISBN 0-7636-2475-6

10 9 8 7 6 5 4 3 2 1

Printed in Singapore

This book was typeset in Futura T.
The illustrations were done in acrylic.

Candlewick Press
2067 Massachusetts Avenue
Cambridge, Massachusetts 02140

visit us at www.candlewick.com

NG!

Sean Taylor

illustrated by

Bruce Ingman

CANDLEWICK PRESS
DGE, MASSACHUSETTS

A terrible thing happened to
the Great Elastic Marvel,
five times World Trampolining Champion
(sometimes known as the Man with Rubber Legs,
the Jumping Master).
As he was practicing his deadly difficult,
quadruple headfirst flip . . .

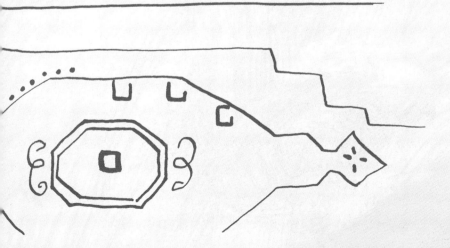

he didn't notice that the window was open.
And he flipped headfirst out of it.

His son, Felix, was way too busy to notice
what had happened.

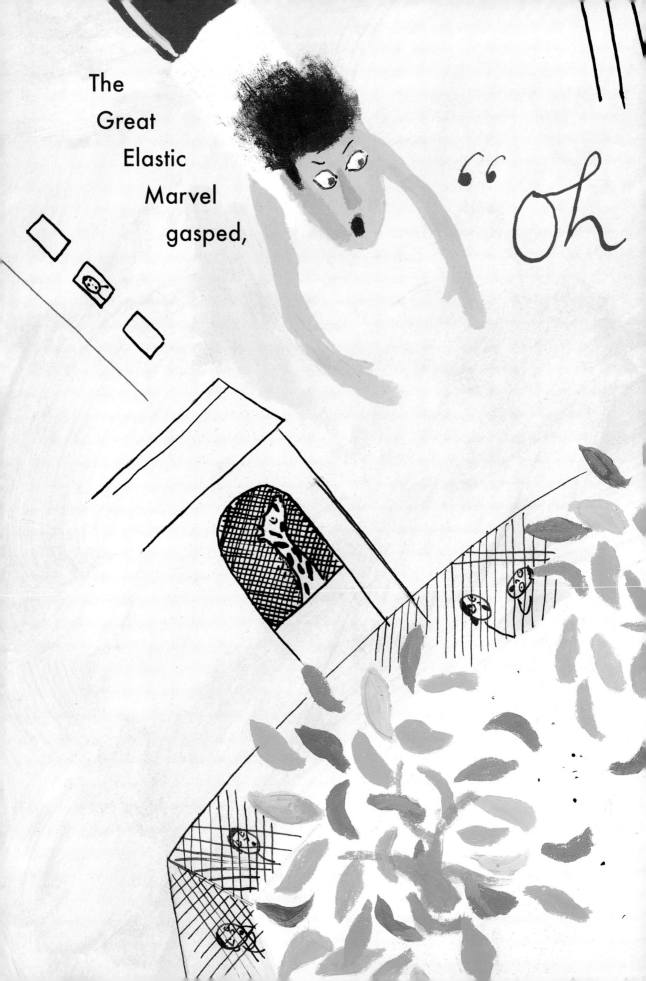

The Great Elastic Marvel gasped, "Oh

my giddy gosh!"

as he found himself falling past
windows and down toward
the lion house of the city zoo.

The lions
looked up hungrily
as he tumbled toward them.

But by some miracle,
the Great Elastic Marvel
landed on the springy
branch of a tree,
did a half twist,

then with a wave to the onlooking children, called,

"Hooplah!"

and bounced back into the sky.

BOI

NG!

When he looked down again,
the Great Elastic Marvel
(sometimes known as the Man
with Rubber Legs, the Jumping Master)
gasped,

"Holy

moly!"

because below him was the cold,
dark water of the river.
He thought his time had come.

But as luck would have it,
a barge carrying 450 mattresses
chugged out from under the bridge.
The Great Elastic Marvel did
a seat drop into the middle
of the mattresses.

Then with a crisp salute to the captain
of the barge, he called,

"Hup!"

and bounced
back into the sky.

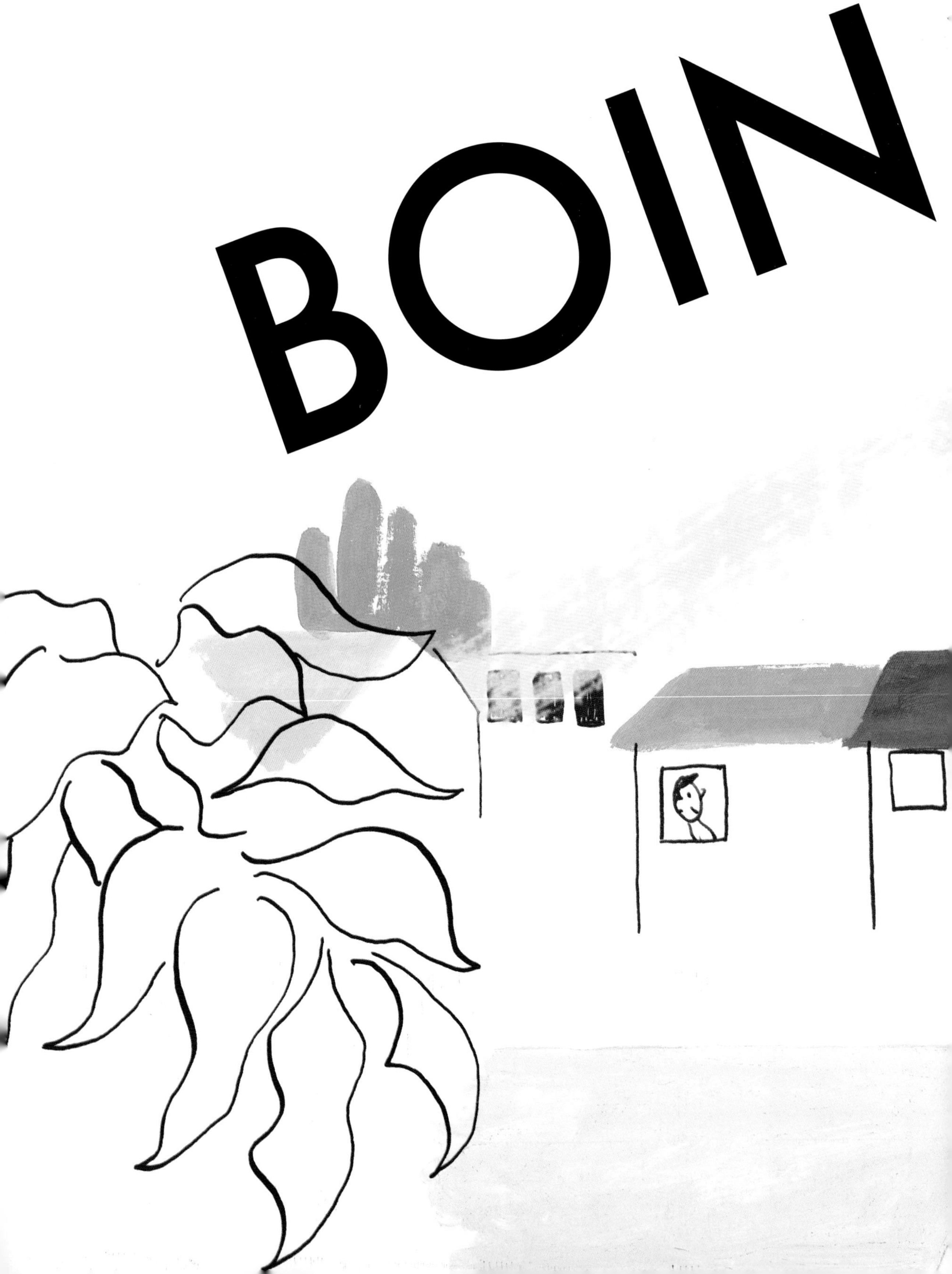
BOIN

G!

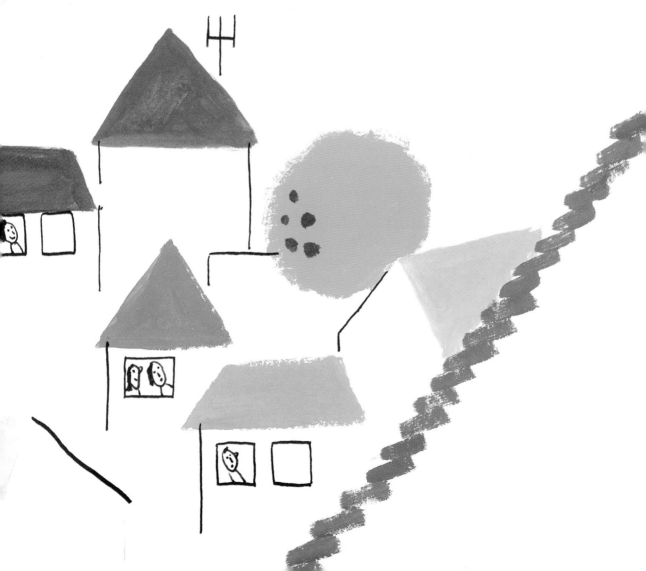

Though he was hoping for a safe landing, it wasn't to be. Looking down again, he gasped,

"O'Reilly!"

because there
were the glinting
lines of the high-speed
railway track.
With thoughts of his
rubber legs being cut
clean away by a train
traveling at 160 miles per
hour, he whistled downward.

BU

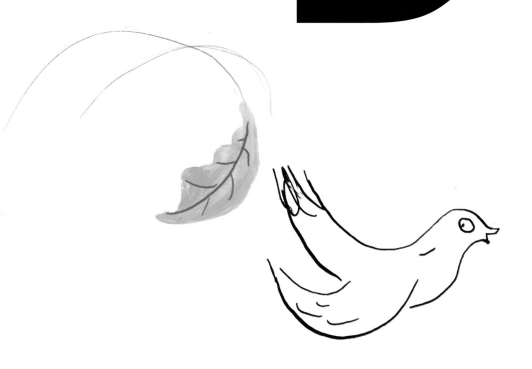

by some blessing from no one knows where,
a gust of wind blew the Great Elastic Marvel
onto the telephone wires, and with a call of

"Kay!"

he performed a rare triple back twist
and bounced back up into the sunshine.

When he looked down again,
he could see the rooftops of the old town.

imstone and Ginger!"

he gasped,
certain that he'd be
spiked like a kebab
on a television antenna.

But by some happy chance,
he fell into an alley just as Madame Petit Four
pulled down the striped awning of her patisserie.
With a deft hitch kick, the Great Elastic Marvel
(sometimes known as the Man with Rubber Legs,
the Jumping Master) sank into the awning.

Then with a
piked jump,

a barrel roll,

and a cry of

out he came.

"watch your head,
madame petit four!"

HOSPITAL

BOIN

G!

There was such a spring
in Madame Petit Four's awning
that the Great Elastic Marvel
was sent spinning over the
hospital, over the vegetable
market and the town hall . . .

until
he found
himself
looking
down
on the
benches
and
trees
of the
park.

Directly below, to his horror,
was the symphony orchestra
playing an open-air concert.

The piano
boomed.

The violins
quivered.

The trumpets
gleamed.

he gasped,
plummeting
downward.

But by some stroke of fortune,
the Great Elastic Marvel landed right
in the middle of a kettledrum, did a
side somersault, a cheeky tilt twist, called,

"Hah!"

and without causing the orchestra to skip a beat, rose majestically back into the air.

BO

Up he sailed, hurtling straight toward the windows of a tall building.

And he seemed to recognize that building.

By some amazing fluke,
it was the very apartment building where he lived!
All it took was a back twist, a tuck,
a side straddle . . .

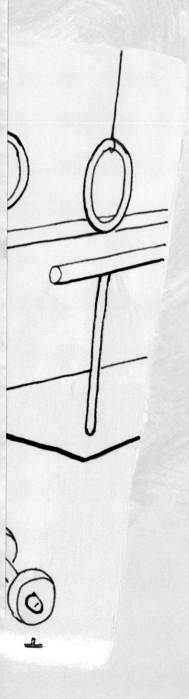

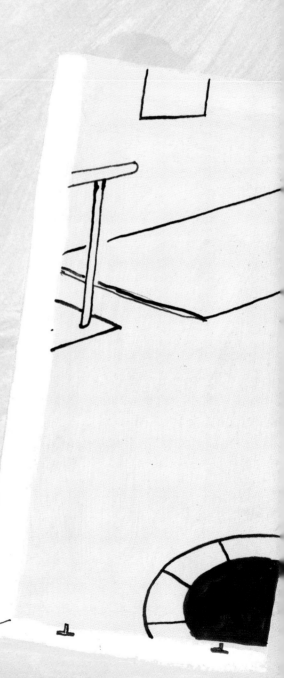

and the Great Elastic Marvel flew in through
the window of his very own apartment.

There was Felix. There was his trampoline,
poised to give him a safe landing.

But by an extraordinary stroke of bad luck, his shoelace snagged on the window catch. And with a gasp of

"Oh dear!"

he missed the
trampoline.

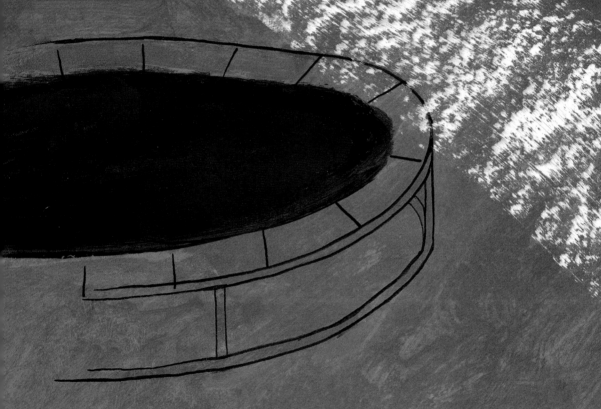

G!

"That jump needs some practice, Dad," said Felix.

And that was how the Great Elastic Marvel
(sometimes known as the Man with Rubber Legs,
the Jumping Master)
also became known as the Man with Rubber Legs
and His Bottom in Plaster.

The
Ela

But do you think it stopped him?